The Chimpanzees of Happytown

Giles Andreae

Illustrated by
Guy Parker-Rees

ORCHARD BOOKS

There was a town not far from here
Called Drabsville, USA,
Where all the houses looked the same
And all of them were grey.

There were no parks to play in.

There were no trees at all.

Now, Chutney was a traveller.
He travelled far and wide.
And he came home with a box one day,
Which had a seed inside.

He planted it

and watered it

And watched it slowly grow –

Until, one day, the mayor looked down
And shouted, "No,
 NO,
  NO!"

From way up in his palace
He had spotted Chutney's seed.
And now he bellowed, "Chop it down!
Destroy that ghastly weed!"

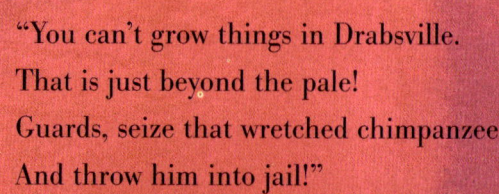

"You can't grow things in Drabsville.
That is just beyond the pale!
Guards, seize that wretched chimpanzee
And throw him into jail!"

So Chutney went to prison,
Where his cell was cold and bare.
And the mayor left for his winter break
To catch some country air.

But meanwhile, back at Chutney's house,
The boy and girl next door

Said, "We must water Chutney's seed

And make it grow once more."

And, with the children's love and care,
It wasn't very long
Before the seed stretched out its shoots
And grew up tall and strong.

It gave him strength.

It gave him hope.

It made him happy too.

And when, at last, they let him out
He said, "There's work to do!"

HAPPY TOWN

The chimpanzees fell silent.
These were stirring words to hear.
"He's right," they said. "That Chutney's right!"
And they began to cheer.

"I'm going to paint mine pink," one said.
"That's what I'm going to do.

Then I'm going to climb up on the roof
And paint the chimney blue!"

"My windows will look fabulous
Without those iron bars,
And the walls will be a symphony
Of flowers and hearts and stars!"

Then Chutney stopped and looked up
At the palace of the mayor.
"The children need a place to play,"
He said. "Let's build it there."

And loads of other things.

"Let's have a party," Chutney said,
"With yummy things to eat!"
There were sausages and ice cream.
There was dancing in the street.

And everyone was happy now
Except, of course, the mayor,
Who came back to his palace.
But his palace wasn't there.

"What's happened here?" he said. "Enough!
Guards, seize them, every one!"
But the guards, of course, just laughed
And said, "We're having too much fun!"

So they put the mayor in prison,
Where he settled in quite well –

Until, one day,
the new mayor came
And opened up his cell.

Mayor Chutney said, "You see my tree?
Well, now I hope you know
That everything that we cut down
Will find a way to grow."

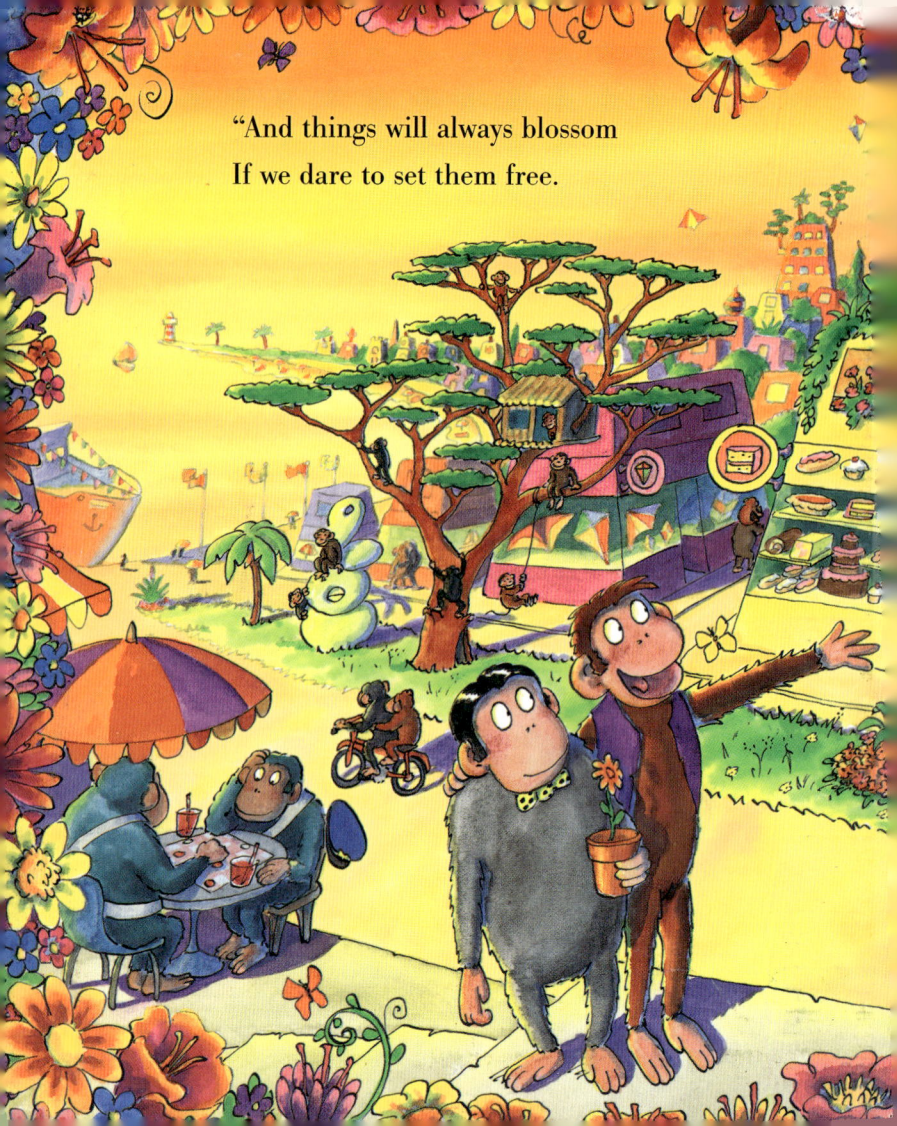

"And things will always blossom
If we dare to set them free.

GIRAFFES CAN'T DANCE

Giles Andreae

illustrated by Guy Parker-Rees

ORCHARD BOOKS

Gerald was a tall giraffe
Whose neck was long and slim,
But his knees were awfully bandy
And his legs were rather thin.

JUNGLE DANCE

And this year when the day arrived
Poor Gerald felt so sad,
Because when it came to dancing
He was really very bad.

The lions danced a tango
Which was elegant and bold.

The chimps all did a cha-cha
With a very latin feel,

And eight baboons then teamed up For a splendid Scottish reel.

Gerald swallowed bravely
As he walked towards the floor,
But the lions saw him coming
And they soon began to roar.

"Hey, look at clumsy Gerald,"
The animals all laughed,
"Giraffes can't dance, you silly fool,
Oh Gerald, don't be daft!"

Gerald simply froze up,
He was rooted to the spot.
"They're right," he thought, "I'm useless,
Oh, I feel like such a clot."

So he crept off from the dancefloor
And he started walking home,
He'd never felt so sad before
So sad and so alone.

Then he found a little clearing
And he looked up at the sky,
"The moon can be so beautiful,"
He whispered with a sigh.

"Excuse me!" coughed a cricket
Who'd seen Gerald earlier on,
"But sometimes when you're different
You just need a different song."

"Listen to the swaying grass
And listen to the trees,
To me the sweetest music
Is those branches in the breeze.

"So imagine that that lovely moon
Is playing just for you,
Everything makes music
If you really want it to."

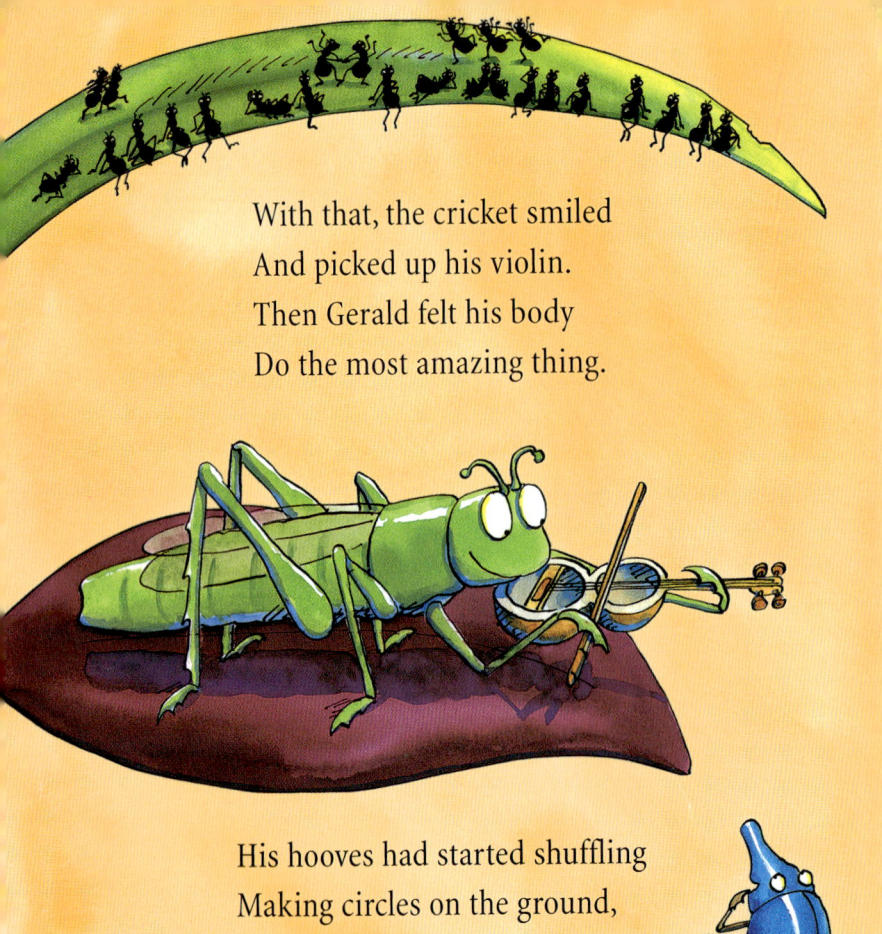

With that, the cricket smiled
And picked up his violin.
Then Gerald felt his body
Do the most amazing thing.

His hooves had started shuffling
Making circles on the ground,
His neck was gently swaying
And his tail was swishing round.

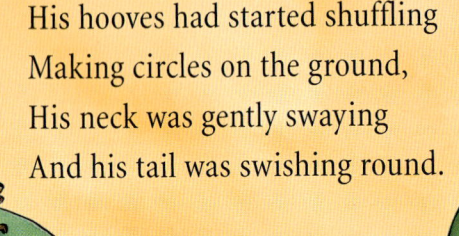

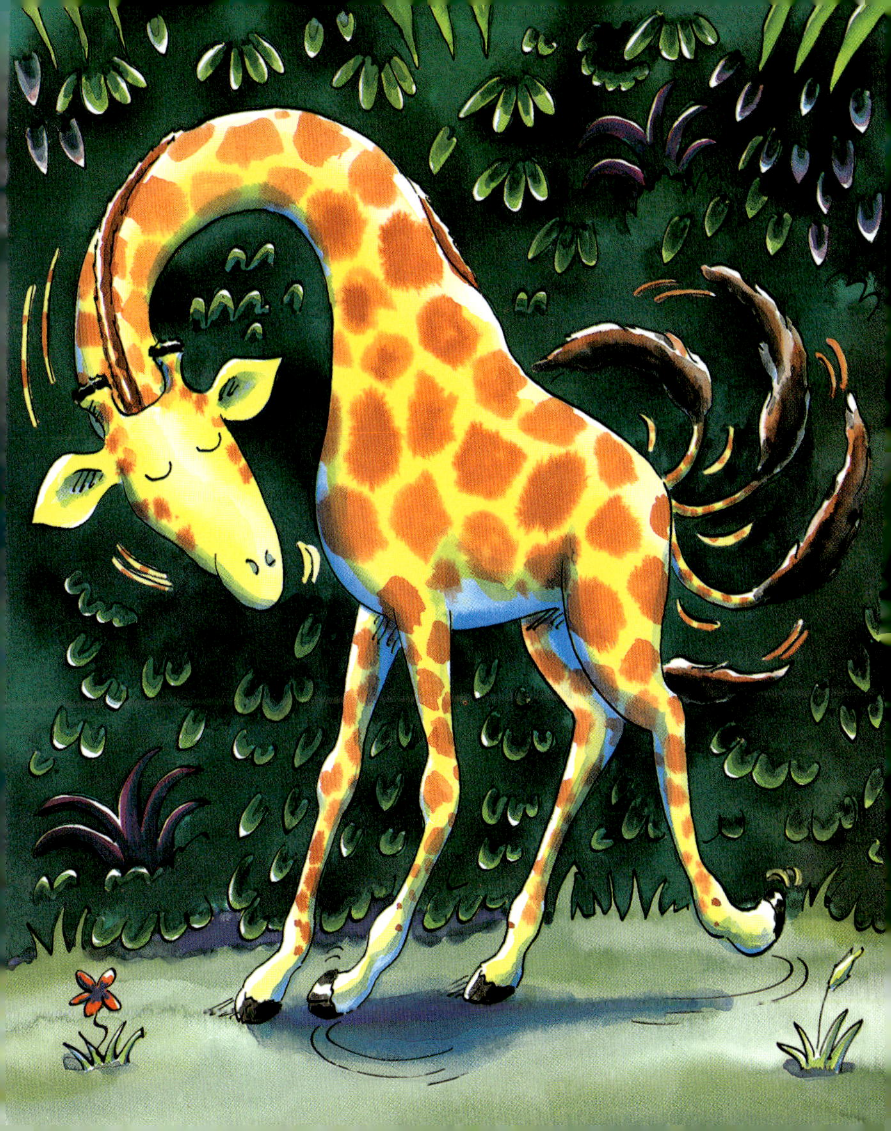

He threw his arms out sideways
And he swung them everywhere,
Then he did a backwards somersault
And leapt up in the air.

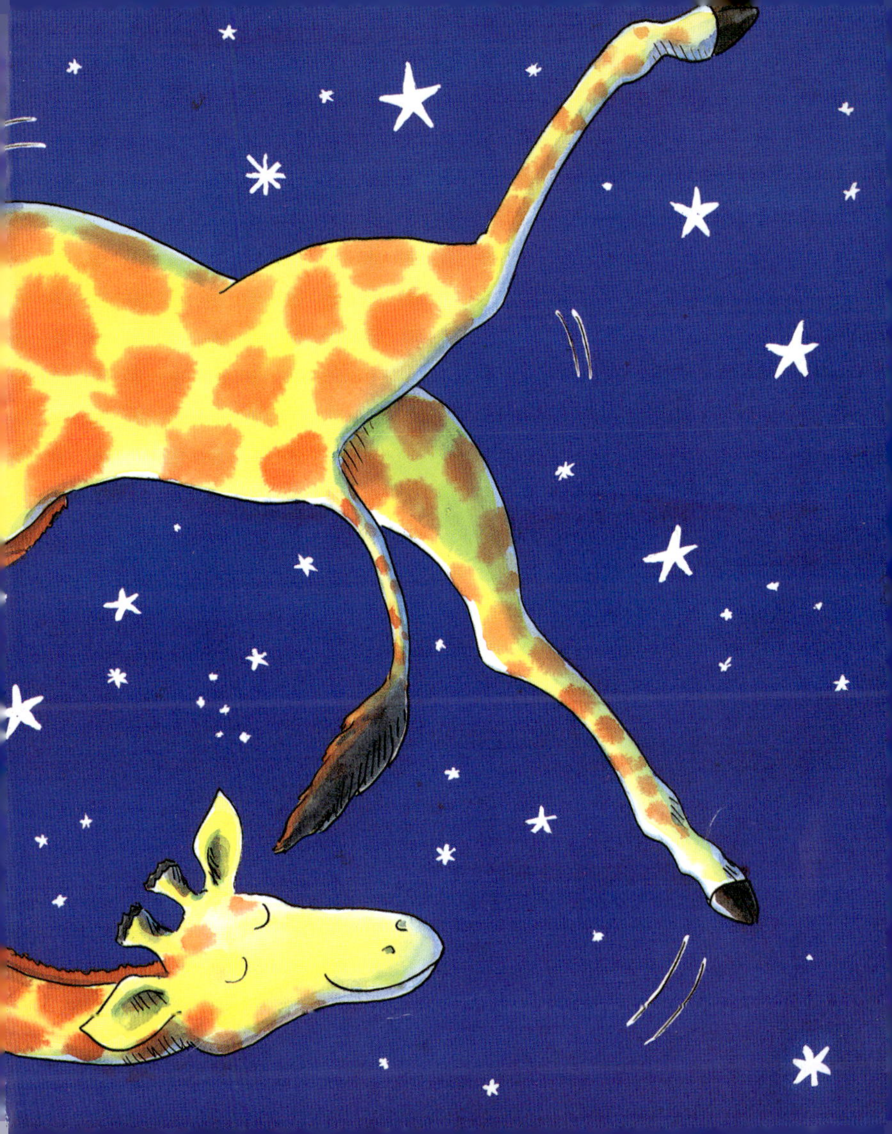

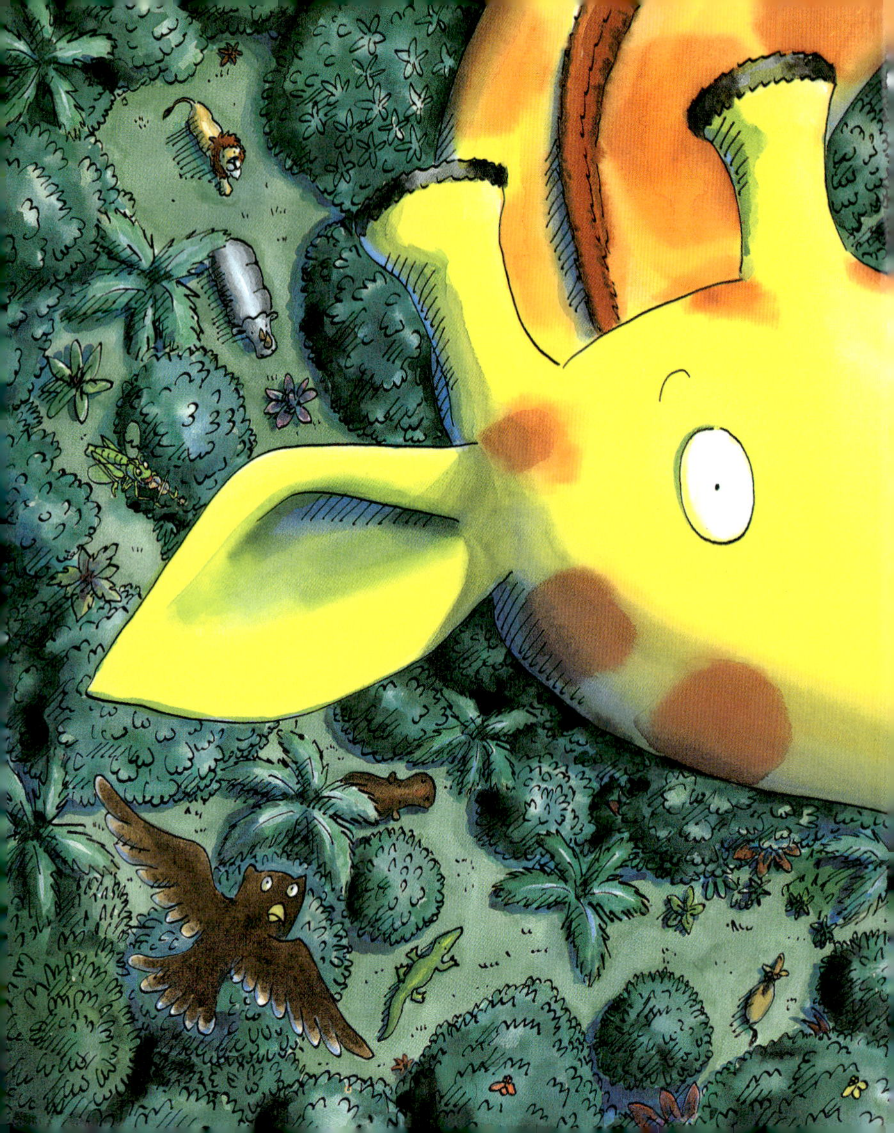

Gerald felt so wonderful
His mouth was open wide,
"I am dancing! Yes, I'm dancing!
I AM DANCING!" Gerald cried.

Then one by one each animal
Who'd been there at the dance
Arrived while Gerald boogied on
And watched him quite entranced.

They shouted, "It's a miracle!
We must be in a dream,
Gerald's the best dancer
That we've ever ever seen!"

"How is it you can dance like that?
Please, Gerald, tell us how."
But Gerald simply twizzled round
And finished with a bow.

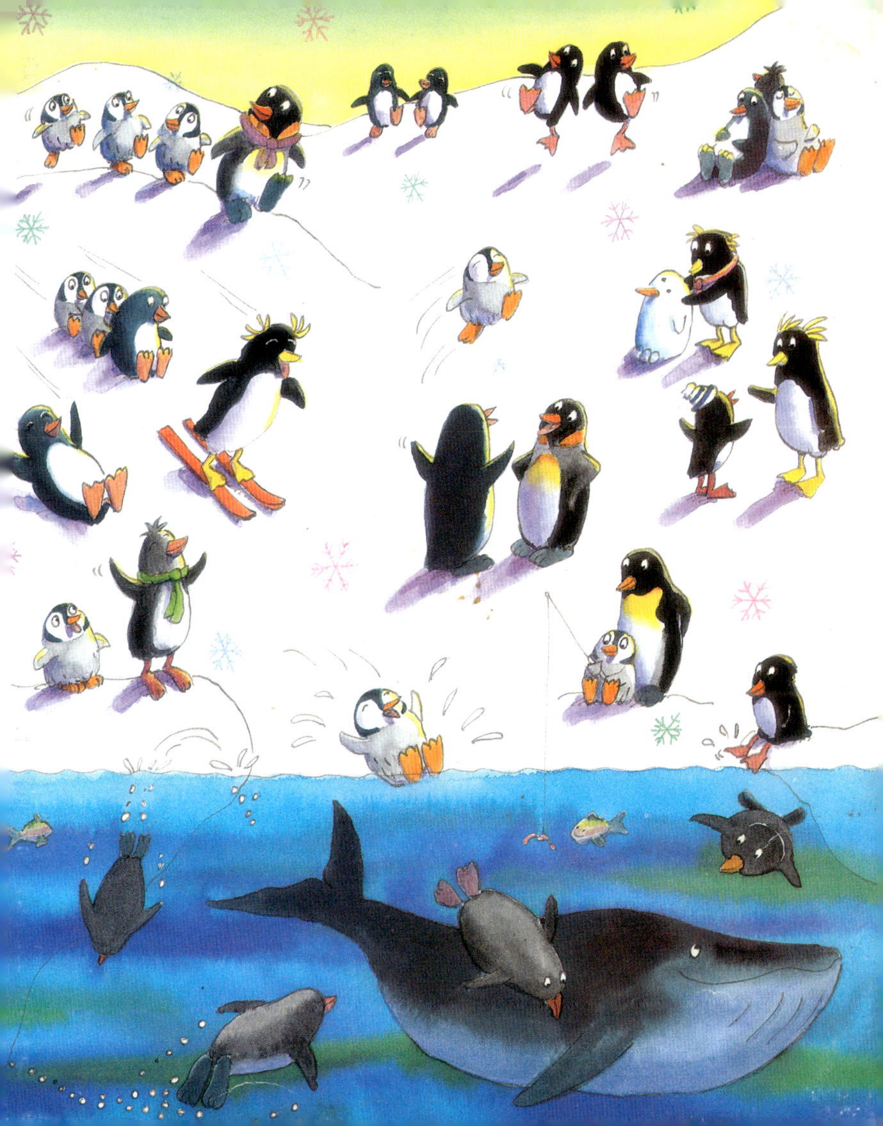

For Wendy Cooling, Polar Explorer.
Warm wishes — T.M.

For Bump,
with love — G.P-R

ORCHARD BOOKS
338 Euston Road, London NW1 3BH
Orchard Books Australia
Level 17/207 Kent Street, Sydney, NSW 2000

First published in 2007 by Orchard Books
First published in paperback in 2008
This edition published in 2008

Text © Tony Mitton 2007
Illustrations © Guy Parker-Rees 2007

The rights of Tony Mitton to be identified as the author
and of Guy Parker-Rees to be identified as the illustrator
of this work have been asserted by them in accordance
with the Copyright, Designs and Patents Act, 1988.

A CIP catalogue record for this book is available from the British Library.

1 3 5 7 9 10 8 6 4 2

Printed in China

Orchard Books is a division of Hachette Children's Books,
an Hachette Livre UK company.
www.hachettelivre.co.uk

Perky Little Penguins

Tony Mitton   **Guy Parker-Rees**

ORCHARD BOOKS

Perky little penguins coming out to play,

looking for their playmates...

here they are – hooray!

Lots of little penguins skimming through the snow, slipping on the slidy ice, squeaking as they go.

Perky little penguins in the wintry weather —

that's how penguins like to play, **waddling** round together.

Perky little penguins make a shiny slide. "Wheeeee!" pipe the penguins. "What a whizzy ride!"

Perky little penguins in the wintry weather — that's how penguins like to play, sliding down together.

Perky little penguins,
as they jump about,
make a squeaky, shrieky noise —
what a squabbly **shout!**

Perky little penguins
are hungry for their lunch, 
so off they go to look for it,
in a busy bunch.

Perky little penguins in the wintry weather — that's how penguins look for lunch, **leaping** out together.

Eager little penguins jumping in the sea,

"**Yay!**" shriek the penguins. "That's the place to be!"

They swirl about, they whirl about, splashy, sploshy, splish.

They curl about, they twirl about, catching tasty fish.

Perky little penguins in the wintry weather — that's how penguins like to lunch, **whirling** round together.

But what's this on the ice floe?

A little ball of fur?

A sobbing baby seal pup!

Whatever's wrong with her?

"Tell us, baby seal pup,

have you come far?

You're looking rather frightened.

Have you lost your ma?"

"She saw some fish go swimming by and dived into the sea. The ice floe we were resting on went drifting off with me!"

"Don't worry, baby seal pup, we're sure she's on her way.

But why not, while you're waiting, watch us as we play?"

All the little penguins try to cheer her up.

And soon she seems much happier, a playful little pup!

The penguins do a dippy dance
with silly jigs and wriggles.

And soon the little seal pup
is full of grins and giggles.

Perky little penguins in the wintry weather — that's how penguins like to play, **messing** round together.

But what's that in the water?
Help, it's coming near!
It's speedy and it's shadowy.
It fills them all with fear.

It's streaking straight towards them.
It leaps upon the ice . . .

Look, it's Seal Pup's mother. Isn't that nice!

Seal Pup calls to Mama
with a squeaky little yelp.
Then Mama thanks the penguins
for their kindness and their help.

Mama Seal takes Seal Pup.

They slowly swim away.

Then the penguins realise it's time to end their day.

Perky little penguins,
how sleepily they go —
waddling and **yawning**,
through the ice and snow.

Home they go together,
back to Mum and Dad.
They tell them all the things they've done
and all the fun they've had.

Sleepy little penguins in a happy huddle — that's how penguins like to rest.

What a cosy cuddle!

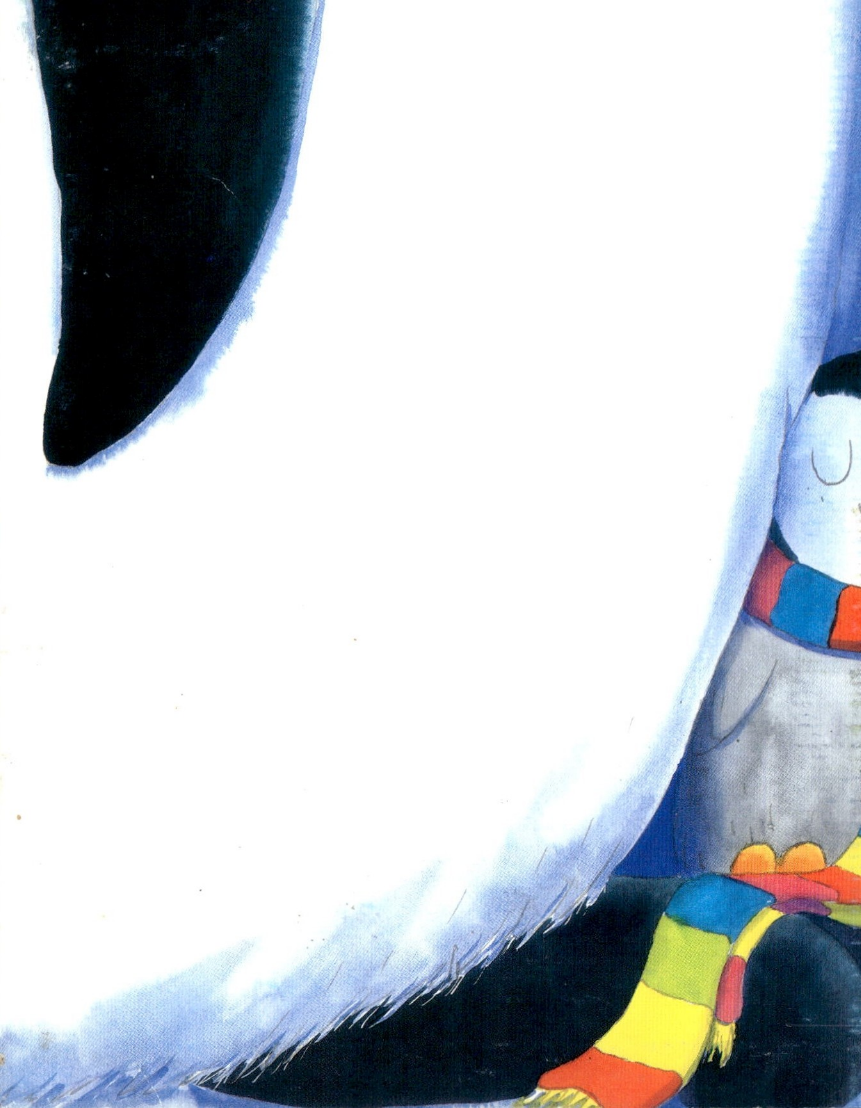

All Afloat on Noah's Boat!

Tony Mitton ♦ Guy Parker-Rees

ORCHARD BOOKS

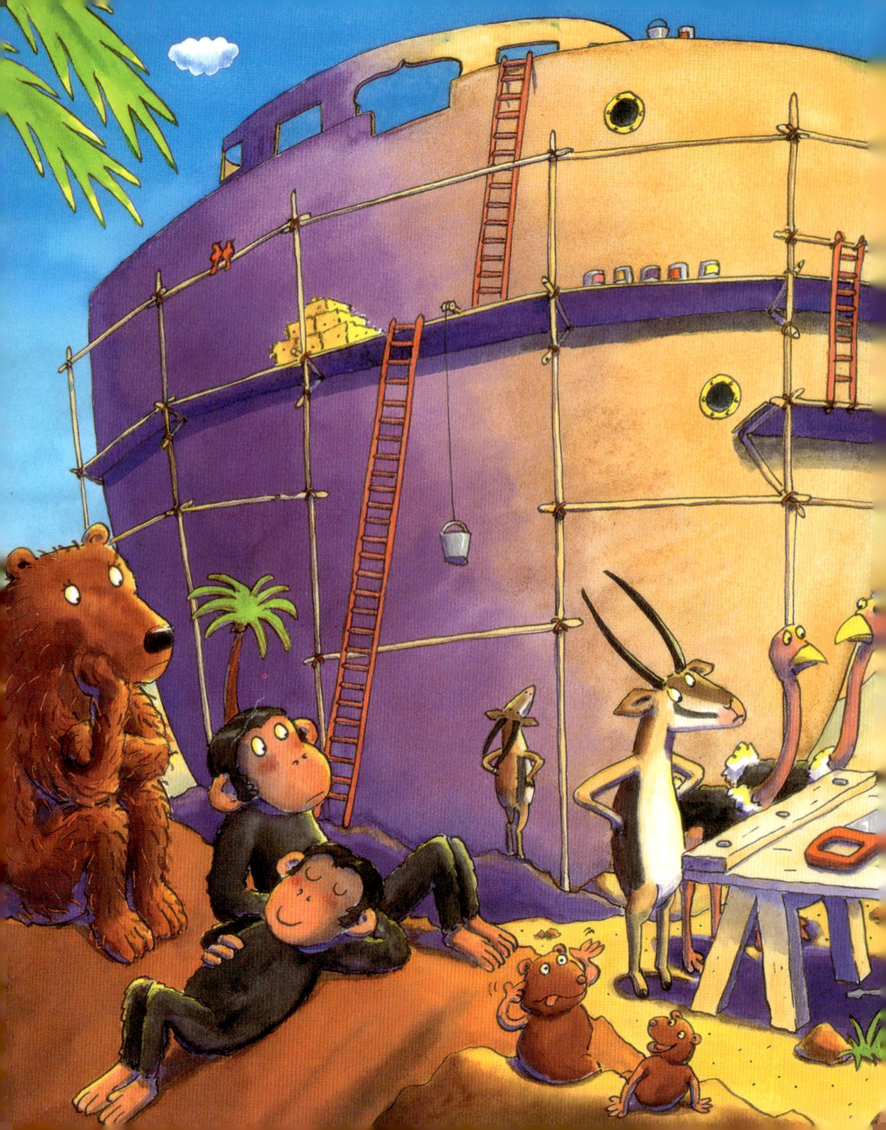

Bang bang, tap tap, chip chip chip.
Noah built a house in the shape of a ship.
He built it **wide** and he built it **tall**.
He built it for creatures **great** and small.

When the rain came down, Noah clanged his bell, crying, "All aboard the Ark Hotel! The ground's getting wet. It'll soon be mud. Come and keep safe from the rising flood."

So, along came the creatures, all in pairs,
flying through the windows, stepping up the stairs,
filling up the Ark with a racket and a row.
There were snakes in the stern
and bears in the bow.

The rain rattled down on the great big boat,

till the water rose and made it float.

All they could see was flood and sky,
but aboard Noah's Ark they were safe and dry.

Well, the days went by and the weeks went past,

and it seemed that the flood would last and last.

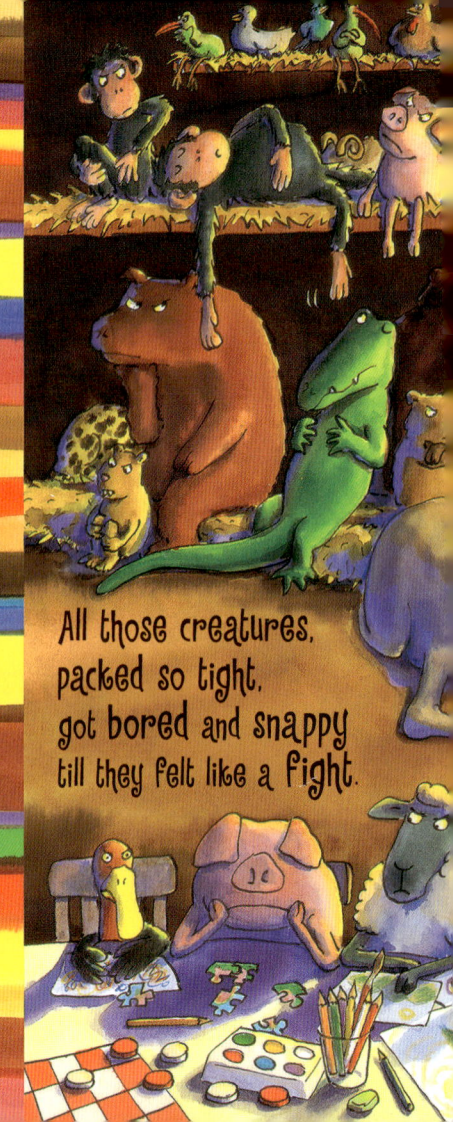

All those creatures, packed so tight, got bored and snappy till they felt like a fight.

The camels got the hump,

and the snakes got the wriggles.

The hyped-up hyenas both got the giggles.

The lions and the leopards turned mean and catty.

And, boy, those rodents sure were ratty!

There were animal tantrums

and insect tiffs,

and the birds nearly came to feathery biffs.

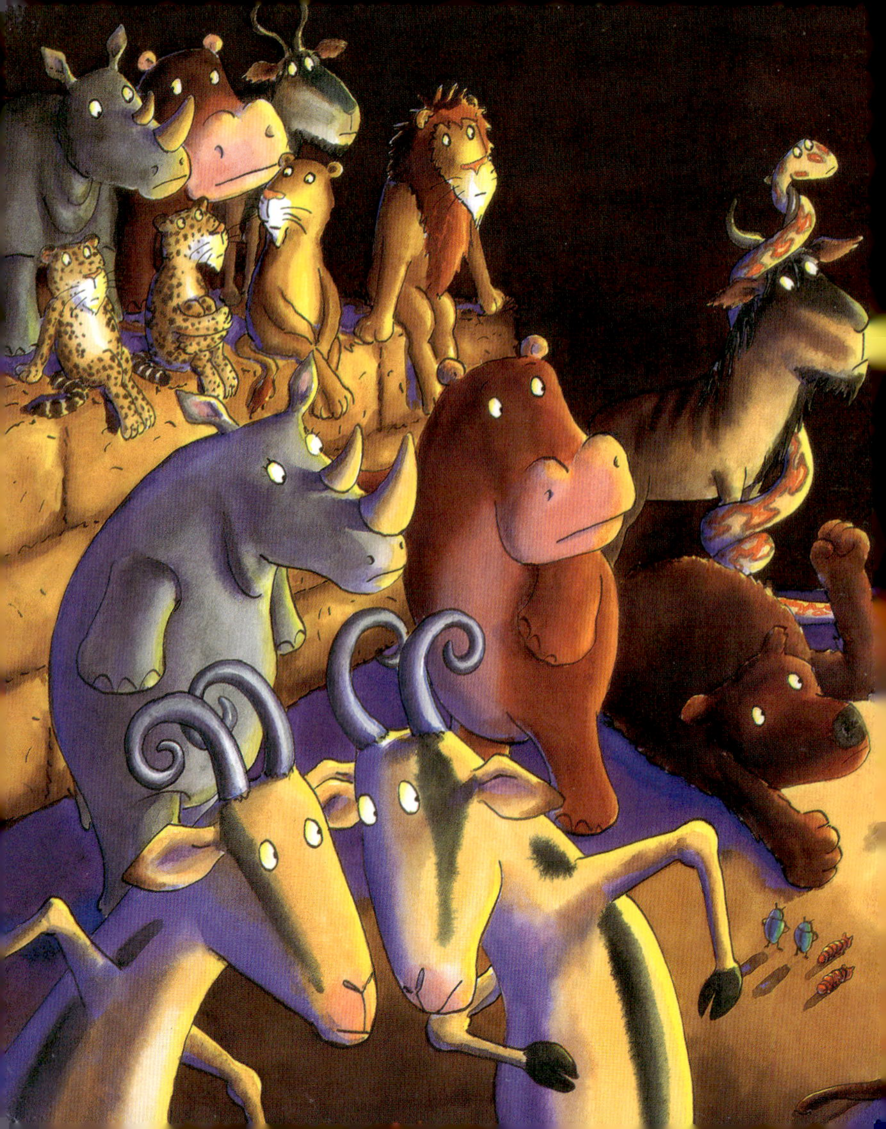

So, Noah stood up, saying,
"Hush and hark!
Any more fuss and you're off my Ark!

The rain's stopped falling,
but the flood's not done,
So, while we're here, let's have some fun.
We'll all get ready for a Talent Show.
You can all do something, isn't that so?"

Clever old Noah.
That did the trick.
There were no more quarrels
or fights to pick.

When at last it was time
to begin the show,
old Noah said, "Well?
Are you ready?

So, the animals came on two by two, to show the things that they could do.

Go!"

The frogs sprang on doing hyper-hops.

They **flipped** all over the **table tops.**

The toucans played a **rhythmic** peck, with **tapping** beaks, upon the deck.

The elephants **dipped** their trunks in the sea and blew high fountains - ready?

Wheeeeeeeee!

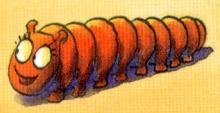

But nobody heard
the caterpillars croon.

"We're wrapping ourselves
in a tight cocoon."

The snakes both **tied** themselves in **knots**.

The leopards **wiggled** all their spots.

Oh, what a **rumpus!**

Oh, what a **row!**

That Talent Show got **busy** now!

But the poor little caterpillars lay quite still, all wrapped up on the windowsill.

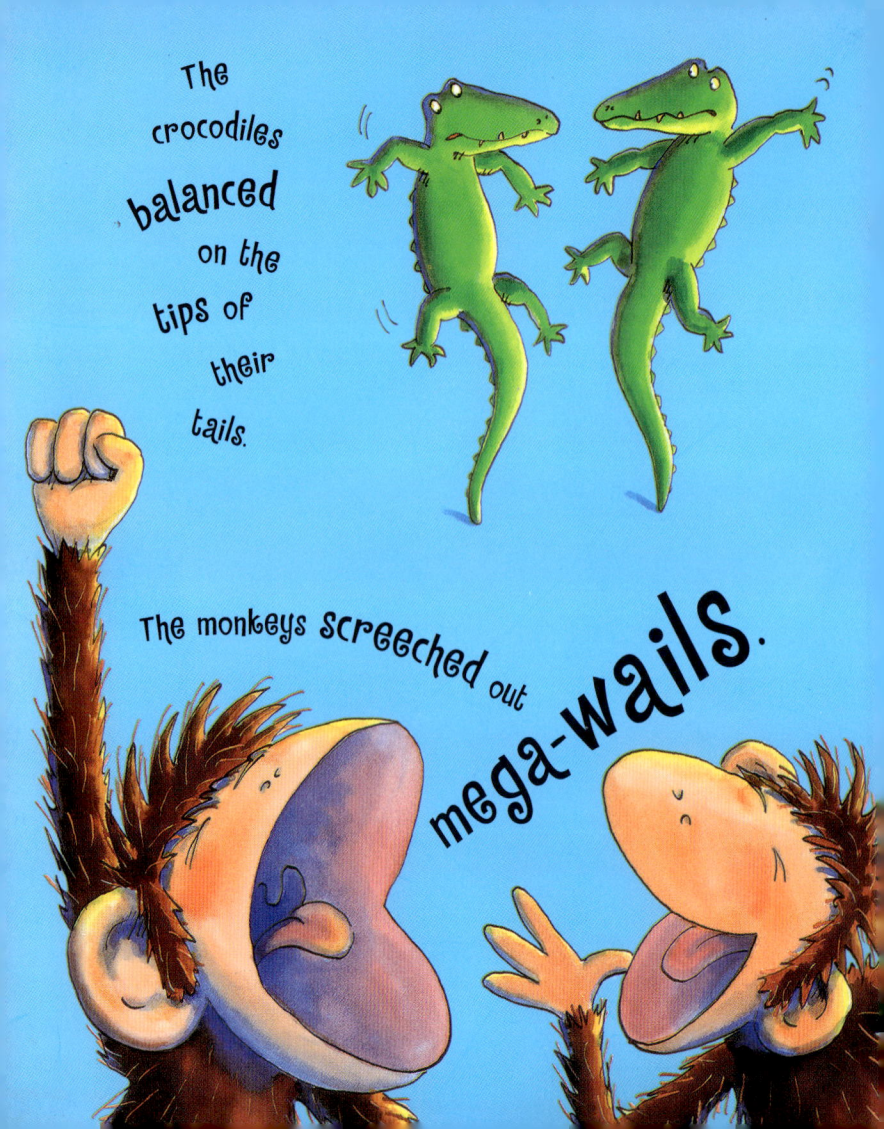

The crocodiles **balanced** on the tips of their tails.

The monkeys **screeched** out **mega-wails.**

The Talent Show was such a ball, there's not the space to tell it all.

And the caterpillars thought, "They're all so good. We'd both join in if we only could."

But when the show was nearly through, Noah whispered, "One more act to do..."

Each caterpillar's tight cocoon looked like it might crack open soon . . .

Then out they burst! Surprise! Surprise!

They'd both turned into **butterflies!**

They spread their brilliant wings out wide and every single creature sighed.

"They're **beautiful!**" said Noah. "Oh, my!
They've opened up their wings to fly.
But look – out there the water's **gone!**
That means there's **land** to live upon."